To Harriet and Cecily.
Dream big and be happy! – T.P.

To Gill, for the digging x – C.P.

BLOOMSBURY CHILDREN'S BOOKS
Bloomsbury Publishing Plc
50 Bedford Square, London, WC1B 3DP, UK

BLOOMSBURY, BLOOMSBURY CHILDREN'S BOOKS and the Diana logo are trademarks of Bloomsbury Publishing Plc

First published in Great Britain in 2021 by Bloomsbury Publishing Plc

Text copyright © Tom Percival 2021
Illustrations copyright © Christine Pym 2021

Tom Percival and Christine Pym have asserted their rights under the Copyright, Designs and Patents Act, 1988,
to be identified as the Author and Illustrator of this work

A catalogue record for this book is available from the British Library

ISBN 978 1 4088 9281 7 (HB)
ISBN 978 1 4088 9282 4 (PB)
ISBN 978 1 4088 9280 0 (eBook)

1 3 5 7 9 10 8 6 4 2

Printed and bound in China by Leo Paper Products, Heshan, Guangdong

All papers used by Bloomsbury Publishing Plc are natural, recyclable products from wood grown in well managed forests.
The manufacturing processes conform to the environmental regulations of the country of origin.

To find out more about our authors and books visit www.bloomsbury.com and sign up for our newsletters

Dream BIG, Little Mole

BLOOMSBURY
CHILDREN'S BOOKS
LONDON   OXFORD   NEW YORK   NEW DELHI   SYDNEY

WRITTEN BY
Tom Percival

ILLUSTRATED BY
Christine Pym

Up on a hillside, early one morning,
a mole sniffed the air
as a new day was dawning.

She gazed at the birds
as they soared through the sky –
and wished in her heart
that she could fly high.

She watched as the ducks
splashed along in the water,
but Mole couldn't swim
because no one had taught her.

She saw Grasshopper leap . . .

and Squirrel climb high.

"I wish I could do that,"
she said with a sigh.

Owl heard the mole's sigh and flew down from her tree.

"Just be who you are," said the owl.
"THAT'S the key!"

"Dream BIG,
Little Mole.
Be brilliant.
Be YOU!"

Then off the owl flapped with a loud twit-twoo.

Mole tried to dream big, but her thoughts were a blur.
Nothing she dreamt up felt quite right for her.

Until something struck her.

She cried, "Owl's so clever!
My skill is to DIG . . ."

"The biggest hole
EVER!"

She dug deep through the soil,
so fast and so keen.

Her hole would be

BIGGER

than any yet seen!

She dug down ever deeper,
through mud and
past rocks . . .

And fell through the roof
of a flute-playing fox!

"Well, thank YOU!" said Fox
(although not very kindly).
"I thought that the WORST
of this week was behind me.

My friend moved away,
now I'm here all alone.
And to make matters WORSE –
you've just RUINED
my home!"

"I'm sorry," said Mole.
"I don't know what to say!"

But Fox rolled his eyes
and just shooed her away.

So Mole tunnelled on, feeling slightly forlorn,
until a voice cried,
"You've just RUINED my lawn!"

Mole had dug up into somebody's garden.
"I'm sorry," she said.
"I DO beg your pardon."

"First my hose gets a hole,"
said Hedgehog, distressed.
"And now look what you've done –
you've made such a MESS!"

Mole repeated, "I'm sorry,"
but there came no reply . . .

So she went on her way . . .

with a tear in her eye.

Up above ground,
   Rabbit ran without care.
He was watching his kite
   bob along through the air.

Then he tripped on some mud
Mole had dug from the ground,
   and his kite flew away
      without making a sound.

Mole watched as the kite
floated off, drifting free.
Then it got tangled
high up in a tree.

Rabbit started to cry,
and then scurried away.
leaving Mole all alone –
this WASN'T her day!

Poor little Mole had a sad, heavy heart.
It seemed her BIG dream was now falling apart.
She'd wanted to dig – make the world's BEST hole.
But she'd made people sad
and that wasn't her goal.

"No more!"
she exclaimed.
"I will give up
for good."

Then a beautiful melody rang through the wood!

She followed the tune, digging carefully on, until . . . .

She met Otter, who asked what was wrong.

When Mole explained,

Otter sang, "Just keep on going!
You WILL dig your hole. This is no time for slowing!"

"I've practised a LOT to sing clear and true.
And practice makes perfect
whatever you do!"

So Mole dug back down
    till her paws felt all soggy,
and she noticed the ground
    was now feeling quite boggy.

"Oh, no!" panicked Mole,
    her whiskers a-quiver.
She seemed to have dug through . . .

The bank of a river!

The water gushed out, flowing

faster and faster!

Had Little Mole's dream
become a DISASTER?

When she popped above ground,
Mole was feeling quite tense.
Her digging had set off
a chain of events.

The water GUSHED out,
shooting high up a tree,
in a powerful jet
that set Rabbit's
kite free.

In Hedgehog's dry garden,
a shower
of
r a i n . . .

meant everything started
to grow once again.

From the top
of a spout,
Fox heard Otter's
sweet song . . .

And, in no time at all, he was playing along.

All the problems were solved, and Mole felt so glad.
She'd brought strangers together –
they were no longer **sad**!

They laughed as they worked
to clear everything up.

And Mole marvelled at what
can come out of bad luck.

"Well, WHAT an adventure!"
said Owl. "In the end,
it seems that YOUR talent is . . .